Mrs Turnip's Treasure

Mrs Turnip's Treasure

ANNE THORNE

Illustrated by Nick Ward

SCRIPTURE UNION

© Anne Thorne 1997

First published 1997

Scripture Union, 207–209 Queensway, Bletchley, Milton Keynes,
MK2 2EB, England.

ISBN 1 85999 052 5

British Library Cataloguing-in-Publication Data.
A catalogue record of this book is available from the British
Library.

Printed and bound in Great Britain by Cox & Wyman Ltd,
Reading.

Contents

For Toby the dog.

For Edna.

Chapter 1

Puppy Problem

I wonder if you've ever wanted something very, very much? So much that it felt as if you hurt all over? Adam felt like that about a puppy. Ever since he could remember, Adam had wanted one of his own. He wanted one so much that when he closed his eyes he could almost feel a tiny puppy, warm and soft in his arms. When it was very small he would look after it carefully. When it was older they could go for walks, and run together, and play catch.

Every Christmas he asked for a puppy and every birthday it was the first thing on his present list. Every time he asked, his mum and dad said, "Not yet, Adam, wait until you're older. When you're older you can have a puppy of your own."

So Adam waited, and waited and waited ...

It was the first day of school, right after the summer holidays, and Adam was sitting in the hall with the rest of his class. They were looking at the most beautiful dog Adam had ever seen. Its name was Ben and it was a guide dog. Adam's school collected money for *Guide dogs for the Blind* and Ben and his owner had come to say thank you.

At the end of the morning, children crowded around the dog, patting and stroking him. He sat very still, wagging his tail and smiling doggy grins at them all. Adam stayed with Ben so long that he was nearly late for lunch, but at last he had to go.

"Adam!" his friend Mandy called across the dinner hall. "Adam! Come on, I've saved you a place." Adam pushed his way to the table and sat down.

Adam Inchley and Mandy West had been friends for a long time. In fact, they'd been friends ever since their first day at school. They'd arrived wearing the same football shirts: the same number and the same team. Mandy had stared at him and said, "You're wearing my shirt!" and Adam had said, "No I'm not. You're wearing mine!"

People kept coming up to them and saying, "Hello, are you two twins, or something?" That had made Mandy and Adam giggle, because Mandy's hair was black and her eyes were brown, but Adam had fair

hair and his eyes were blue. After all that they just had to be friends.

"I'm starving!" said Mandy, offering one of her crisps to Adam. "I didn't think I was hungry till I sat down. That lovely dog made me forget about everything else."

Adam unpacked his lunch. He picked up a sandwich and bit into it angrily. He swung his legs, kicking his feet against the table. Mandy looked up in surprise.

"What's the matter, Adam?" she asked.

"Seeing Ben made me think about my puppy," said Adam. "Mum and Dad said I could have one when I was older and that was *ages* ago. Just because Richard and Emma are older than me, they don't seem

to notice I'm growing up. It's not fair!"
Richard and Emma were his stepbrother
and stepsister.

"I know what it's like," said Mandy.
"Parents never think you can do anything.
I don't see why they won't let you have a
puppy now. I could help you look after it,
too. That'd be really good!"

Mandy wasn't allowed any pets. Her
family often went to the West Indies in the
holidays. It was always exciting to fly to
another country, but it meant she wasn't
allowed an animal even as small as a
hamster. Mandy didn't have any brothers
or sisters either, but she didn't mind that.

"We'll have to make a plan," said Mandy.
She pushed her lunch box towards Adam.
"Let's have some chocolate cake. It might
help us to think."

"Thanks," said Adam. He helped himself
to a slice of the thick, creamy cake and for
a while they stopped talking.

Mandy liked the idea of Adam having a
puppy because it would be almost as good

as having a dog of her own. Her mother was a doctor, and when she was at work Mandy went to Adam's house. Sometimes, when her parents were away, Mandy stayed with the Inchleys. She enjoyed sharing a room with Adam's stepsister. Emma was fun to be with and she always had time to listen.

"I know," said Mandy, licking the crumbs from her fingers, "why don't you talk to Emma about it? Perhaps *she* could get your mum and dad to let you have a puppy."

"That's a good idea," said Adam. "Let's ask her as soon as we get home."

"We'll have to get her by herself," said Mandy. "That might not be easy if your mum's planning a picnic." The Inchleys' small house was always full of people, and you never knew what was going to happen next. Sometimes Adam's mum would say, "Come on everyone! Let's cook tea on the beach," and off they'd all go, walking the short way to the seaside and carrying things like a camping stove and a frying pan and strings of sausages.

"Then let's hope it's raining, and Emma's on her own," said Adam.

"Yes," said Mandy. "If she is, we'll grab her right away!" Adam was really pleased with their plan. If he had Mandy *and* Emma on his side he might actually get his puppy. He could hardly wait!

Chapter 2

Look at me, I'm being good!

"Emma! Emma! Are you there?" said Adam as soon as they got in from school. "We've got something to ask you!"

"Hello, you two!" called Emma from upstairs. She was in her room listening to music.

"Can we talk to you?" asked Mandy. "Adam needs your help with something."

"Come on in," she said. "What do you want to ask me about?"

"There was a guide dog at school today," Adam began.

"It made Adam think about his puppy," explained Mandy. "He's wanted one for ages."

"Mum and Dad said I could have one when I was grown up, but they still keep telling me to wait," said Adam.

"He wants one now," said Mandy, "so will you talk to them, please? We think they'd listen to you."

"I could try talking to them," said Emma, "but it might not do any good, Adam. I think you'll have to try and *show* them how grown up you are."

"They must know I'm growing," said Adam. "They made an awful fuss when I grew out of my trainers."

"You'll have to show them you've grown sensible, as well," said Emma.

"Hmm," said Adam. "What could I do to show them that?"

"Well, let's think," Emma started counting on her fingers. "One, you could put your football things in the washing. Two, clean your bike. Three, clear up your bedroom."

"It's Richard's room too," Adam protested.

"But you make most of the mess," said Emma. "Richard complains that it oozes over his side. He says he's afraid to touch it in case it bites!"

Adam giggled. "Things do seem to spread out," he admitted.

"You could do the washing-up as well," said Mandy helpfully.

"Thanks!" said Adam. "This isn't going to be easy. I'd better start right away."

All that week Adam worked at being good. He sorted out his bedroom and helped his

mum to clean the car. He dried the dishes and he even let Richard switch the TV programme without making a fuss.

"How's it going?" asked Mandy. It was a week later and they were in the sitting-room, watching his hamster climb up the curtains. "I'm trying really hard," said Adam, rescuing his pet, "but no one's said anything. I hope they notice soon. All this being good's wearing me out!"

"Just keep thinking about that puppy," said Mandy. She watched the hamster sniff around the floor. It seemed to be tasting a rug. "I'll try and get your mum to see how helpful you are." She scooped up the hamster. "Come on, Hammy. Come and have a peanut to eat. A hole in the carpet is just what Adam doesn't need!"

Mrs Inchley called them for tea. It was a bit crowded at the table and Richard and Adam usually complained about each other, but this time Adam pretended not to notice when Richard's elbow dug into his ribs. He volunteered to say grace and, when everyone had said "Amen", he helped to hand things round. When they'd all finished, he and Emma took the empty plates out to the kitchen.

"Have you noticed anything about Adam?" asked Mandy while he was out of the room.

"He does seem a bit quiet," said Mrs Inchley. "Is everything all right at school?"

"Oh yes," said Mandy. "Our teacher keeps saying how *sensible* Adam is."

"I thought he was rather quiet," said his father. He turned to his wife. "Do you think Adam's ill?" he asked. Mandy tried not to giggle.

"I think I'll take his temperature," said Mr Inchley. He went out to the kitchen as Adam walked in. He came back with a thermometer in his hand. When Mandy saw the look on Adam's face she had a struggle not to laugh out loud.

"I'm all right," said Adam, trying to push his father's hand away. "I'm fine, honestly."

Mr Inchley put the plastic strip across Adam's forehead.

"Normal," he read, after a few minutes.

"I told you!" said Adam. "Can I have my pudding now?" He helped himself from a plate of cakes on the table.

"He couldn't eat so much if he was ill," said Richard. "Come on, monster, leave some for the rest of us. I'm going to band practice at church tonight and I need lots of energy to play my guitar."

Soon after they'd finished tea, Mandy's dad called for her.

"Can Adam come to football this Saturday?" he asked. "It's an away match and we won't be back until late. Adam can stay the night with us and we'll meet you at church on Sunday."

"Can I go, Mum? Please?" asked Adam. He loved going to football in the Wests' fast, comfortable car. On the way to the match they sang football songs, and on the way back they stopped for pizza and chips. Best of all was sitting with the other fans, cheering and shouting when their team scored.

"I'm not sure." Mrs Inchley gave Adam her *worried* look. "We think he may be ill. Do you know if anyone's got chickenpox at their school?"

"I don't think so," said Mr West. He winked secretly at Adam. "He looks fine to me."

"I *am* fine." said Adam. "Why doesn't anyone believe me?" and he thought, Why doesn't anyone notice I'm *being good*? They notice fast enough when I'm bad!

Chapter 3

You really must be listening!

Adam was very keen to show his parents he wasn't ill, so after school next day he had a big water-pistol fight in his room. He and his friend Jack had a great time, squirting each other and ducking under the beds. They aimed very carefully, but somehow the water got everywhere. It got all over the bedclothes, and all over the carpet, and all over Richard's homework.

When Adam's mother found out she was really angry. She was especially cross about Richard's spoilt work. Sometimes, sharing a room with his brother was just too difficult, Adam thought.

"Mum was really mad," he told Mandy at school next day. "I'm grounded for two days."

"That's not too bad," said Mandy. "At least they know you're not ill, and you can come to football on Saturday. It would have been awful to miss the match."

"Yes," said Adam, "I'm glad I can go to football, but I'm not any nearer to getting a puppy. Mum and Dad won't listen to me now and all that being good has gone to waste. I just don't know what else I can do."

"I haven't got any ideas, either," said Mandy, "but I'm sure we'll think of something."

Adam had a lot of time to think while he was grounded, but when Friday arrived he still hadn't thought of a way to get his puppy. After school, Adam went to Mandy's house for tea, then they played on her computer until it was time to go to Friday Club. The club was at their church, just for their age group, and they did all kinds of things.

"We're going sailing tonight," said one of the leaders when they arrived. "It'll be the last time this year."

"Sailing's one of my favourite things," said Mandy as they drove to the beach. "I'd love a boat of my own."

When they arrived, the leader gave out life-jackets and reminded them about safety at sea. He put them into groups of three, each with an instructor, and they got into the small boats. It was exciting to cast off and feel the waves slapping against the sides of the boat, and the power of the wind as they hoisted the sail. They had a great time, sitting out on the side to balance the boat and then taking turns to steer.

"That was good fun," said Adam on the way back.

"The race was terrific," said Mandy. "We beat all the other boats."

Back at the church, the leader asked them to be quiet. "Most of Jesus' special friends, his disciples, were ordinary people," he told them. "They knew about ordinary things like sailing and fishing. Jesus had to teach them about special things, like praying, and we can learn from what he said."

He opened the Bible. "Here is what Jesus said. 'Ask, and you will receive; seek, and you will find ...' He's telling us that God is like a loving father. When we pray, we are talking to him. We can even ask him for things."

After this, the leader got them into groups again and each person talked to God. Mandy prayed about her relatives in Jamaica. Adam prayed for a puppy.

"I don't think you can pray for that sort of thing," said Jack, who was in their group.

"Why not?" said Mandy. "Jesus told his friends that God would give them things when they asked. Adam really wants a puppy. He's wanted for one for ages."

Jack shrugged. "I suppose it's all right, then," he said.

"It's nearly time to go," said the leader.

Just then Adam's parents walked into the hall.

"Hello, Mum!" said Adam, "You're early!"

"Dad's here as well," said Mrs Inchley. "We've got something to tell you." Adam looked at his parents. They both looked very happy.

"Your mother's got a job," said Mr Inchley.

"It's at a college," said Mrs Inchley, "so I'll be at home in the school holidays. It means we'll have enough money to move to a bigger house."

Mandy looked worried. "I hope this doesn't mean you'll move away," she said.

"Oh, no," said Mrs Inchley. "We'll just find a house nearby with enough room for us all."

"You can have a bedroom of your own," Mr Inchley told Adam. "No more fighting with Richard, and we've decided something else, as well. Once we're settled in our new house you can have your puppy."

Adam felt his mouth drop open. "Wowww!" he said. He looked at Mandy. She was looking stunned too. They'd only just finished praying. Adam had only just asked for a puppy and he hadn't expected his prayer to be answered so soon. God really must be listening to him!

Chapter 4

Meet Mrs Turnip

This is where we meet Mrs Turnip. If you'd been born with a name like that, you'd probably want your parents to change it before you ever walked through a school gate, if you know what I mean.

Mrs Turnip is quite proud of her unusual name but if you want to giggle at it, go ahead, she wouldn't mind a bit. In fact, if you ever did get to meet her, she'd probably join in, chuckling her lovely, friendly chuckle. All her chins would wobble, her bright little eyes would smile at you, and you would probably like her very much.

Mrs Turnip had a bad leg, and couldn't

walk very far. Most of the time she stayed in her lonely cottage on the marshes, but each Sunday she got a lift to church, and that is where Adam and Mandy met her.

After the service Mrs Turnip usually had a crowd of children around her. They liked listening to the stories she told about her great uncle, who had gone to sea in a ship with sails as red as his beard. He had come back with his pockets full of gold. Some people said he'd been a pirate! Mrs Turnip often showed them things he'd found on his adventures.

"Look what I've got to show you today, m'dears," she said one Sunday.

Putting her hand into her bag she brought out a thick, gold ring. It had a strange looking stone in the middle. "This was a real bullet!" she said. "My great uncle had it made into a ring because ..."

"Mandy!" called Dr West, "Come here! I've got something to ask you."

"Oh, Mum!" Mandy went over to where her parents were waiting. "It was just getting to the interesting bit!" Mandy's mother smiled.

"You can hear the story another time," she said. "Adam's parents are having dinner on the beach and they want to know if we'd like to go with them."

"The beach!" said Mandy "Yes, please."

Having dinner by the sea was great, much better than at home. Mandy rushed back to the group around Mrs Turnip. Adam was telling her about the puppy he was going to have, but when Mandy pulled him away and told him the news, he was keen to be off.

They drove as close to the shore as they

could and everybody helped unload the car. Mr Inchley and Mr West got the barbecue going, while the others changed into swimming things. They ran into the sea, splashing each other and squealing at the cold water.

"It may be our last chance to swim this year," said Mrs Inchley. "The sea will be too cold by the end of September."

"Bet you can't catch me!" said Mandy, splashing Adam.

"Bet I can," said Adam, splashing her back. They all joined in a grand water fight. After a while the smell of cooking began to spread across the beach.

"Come on!" called Mr West. "Dinner's nearly ready." They were very hungry, and got dressed even quicker than they'd got into their swimming things. It was Emma's turn to say "Thank you" to God for their food. It seemed a bit strange, talking to God in the open, but everyone said "Amen".

After dinner they played ball on the sand for a while, then went for a walk. They walked a long way, all along the shore and past Whitstable harbour. Mrs Inchley told Dr and Mr West about her new job.

Adam told Mandy how excited they all were about moving and trying to find a new home. "It would be lovely to live in one like that," he said, pointing to some houses right on the edge of the beach. Instead of a back garden they had the same pebbles and stones as the sea shore, and it was difficult to see where the gardens ended and the beach began.

"This one looks exciting," said Mandy. "It's got a wooden platform around the rooms upstairs, where they face the sea."

"Oh, yes!" said Adam as they got nearer. "There are doors leading to it, from the rooms. I think it's called a balcony."

"And it's got stairs leading down to the beach," said Mandy. "You could sneak out when everyone thought you were in bed." They stopped at the house. It looked as if no one had lived in it for a long time. The windows were covered in dust and the grey, wooden walls needed painting. There was a notice stuck onto one of the walls.

"For Sale," Adam read. The others walked up to Adam and Mandy and they read the notice, too.

"Just look at that!" said Mr Inchley. "They'll never sell that old house. It's right by the sea. Who on earth would want to buy that place?" No one answered. Mr Inchley turned around to see his whole family staring at the house. They were smiling. "Oh, no!" he said. "I don't believe it – you can't want – you don't want to live in a house like that?"

Four heads nodded eagerly. Mr Inchley groaned. "No way," he said. "Absolutely not!"

Chapter 5

Fishing from your bedroom?

One Saturday morning, six weeks later, a van with the words *Do-it-yourself Removals* on the side pulled up outside the old house.

Five people got out, and after a bit of excitement when one of them dropped the key, they unlocked the door and disappeared inside. A short time later a car stopped and a slim, dark haired girl got out.

"I'll see you later," said Dr West, and she drove off. Mandy knocked on the door.

"Hello!" said Mrs Inchley. Her hair was tucked up in a baseball cap and she was holding a dustpan and brush. "Go and find Adam. He's upstairs waiting to show you his new room."

Mandy ran up the steps. "Are you there, Adam?" she called. She could see a bathroom, and a cupboard, and empty bedrooms, but she couldn't see Adam anywhere.

"Hello," said a voice. There was a creaking sound and a large, square hole opened above her head. Adam's face appeared in the opening. "It's a trapdoor,' he grinned. "Come on up!" A rope ladder dropped down in front of Mandy.

"This is amazing!" she said, when she'd climbed to the top and wriggled through the hole. They were in a big room, with a sloping ceiling and little windows that faced the sea. "You can see for *miles*. However did you get your parents to give you this room?"

"I really wanted it," said Adam, "and ever since I've been helping with the car, Mum's treated me like I'm older. She and Dad had a big discussion about it. In the end Dad said, 'All right, but don't blame me when he cracks his head open falling down the hole!' and that was it."

"This is really exciting," said Mandy. "Is that rope ladder the only way up?"

"No," said Adam. "But I think it's the best way. This is the other way." He opened a door in one corner.

"Oh," said Mandy, "it leads straight into the open air." Outside the door there was a little platform, with stairs leading down from it. The stairs led to a balcony, then down to the beach, just as they'd seen on their walk.

"I thought your dad wasn't going to buy this house," said Mandy.

"He didn't want to," said Adam, "but it was the only one we could afford with enough rooms for us all."

Well," said Mandy, "I think it's great. It must have belonged to a smuggler, and this was his escape route."

"I bet the smuggler didn't have to move furniture," said Richard, puffing up the steps. He was holding one end of a bed. His dad was holding the other end.

"We're coming in there," said Mr Inchley. "Don't get in the way, you two."

"Let's go back down the trapdoor!" said

Adam. Mandy slid down the rope ladder very fast. It swung around, making them giggle.

"This is Emma's room," said Adam, when they were down. Her room was underneath Adam's and it had a door that led to the balcony. Mandy opened it and stepped outside. She could hear the splash and slop of waves beating on the pebbles below.

"I think you're really lucky to live here!" she said.

"It'll be great when I get my puppy," said Adam. "We can go down to the beach every morning."

"Adam!" called Mrs Inchley from down-stair. "Is that you? Come and help unload the van with us, please."

For the rest of the day they helped to carry things in from the removal van. Adam had never seen so many boxes, all full of things like shoes and books and stuff from the kitchen.

"It's a good thing all the boxes are labelled," said Mandy.

At lunchtime Dr West brought them sandwiches and coffee, and everyone stopped to eat. They sat in the kitchen, glad to have a break.

"Let's give thanks," said Mr Inchley. "Anyone can join in if they want to. I feel in need of some prayers. Lord," he began, "thank you for all you give us."

"Dear Lord, thank you for moving us so quickly," prayed Mrs Inchley.

Adam prayed, "Thank you for my room, and that I can have a puppy now."

"And now, Lord, thank you for this food," said Richard.

By the end of the day everything was inside. Adam felt he never wanted to see another box, ever. It took them ages to get sorted out, but by Friday evening, when Mandy came to stay, the house began to look like home.

Mandy shared a room with Emma, as usual. She put her things down on a chair then went out onto the balcony. Richard's room was next to Emma's and he and Adam were standing in his doorway, busy with a fishing line.

"This is great!" said Mandy. She went and stood against the wooden railing that went all around the balcony.

"You've all got lots of room now, and you're really close to the sea."

"Dad's a bit worried about the sea coming close to *us*!" said Adam. "It's getting nearer and nearer." The waves were quite near their house. They all had to shout a bit because of the noise of the breakers.

"That's because of the tides," said Richard, casting his line out. "The sea goes in and out twice a day, and that's called 'the tides'. Sometimes the tide is very high, and the sea comes right up the shore."

"Like today," said Mandy. She watched the end of the line disappear under the waves.

"Yes," said Adam, "and Dad's not too happy. He doesn't like water very much." Just then Mr Inchley walked in. "So this is where you all are," he said. "Richard, how much closer is the sea going to come to our house? I don't fancy it sloshing around in the living-room!"

"Don't worry, Dad," said Richard. "This is the highest tide in October, the one

42

tonight. The sea won't reach the house. All those pebbles will stop it."

"Even if it does reach us," said Adam, "it won't matter. This house is made of wood. It'll just float away."

"Like a funny shaped boat," said Mandy.

"Is that supposed to make me feel *better*?" said Mr Inchley. "Well, thank you very much! And what are you up to now? Fishing from your *bedroom*? I don't believe it!"

Chapter 6

Treasure

The sea didn't reach the house, and the next morning everybody was at breakfast as usual. They sat around the big kitchen table, and after they'd given thanks for their meal everyone started to talk.

Richard was telling his dad how good it was to have a room to himself. Mandy was telling Mrs Inchley things that were happening at school. Adam was busy at the cooker, using the grill to make toast. In the middle of all this the telephone rang.

"Would you answer that please, Adam?" asked Mrs Inchley. "You're the nearest."

"I can't leave this or it will burn," said

Adam. Richard got up.

"Hello," he said down the phone.

"Why don't you use the toaster?" Mr Inchley asked Adam.

"Mum said I could do it this way," said Adam. "The toast tastes nicer."

Richard was trying to hear above the noise. "Be quiet you lot!" he shouted. "Sorry, not you," he said down the mouth-piece. "It's my family. Yes ... yes ... er ... what was that? ... yes, all right, we'll be expecting you."

"What was all that about?" asked Mrs Inchley.

"Well," said Richard, "it seemed to be about treasure."

"Treasure!" Everyone looked at Richard. Emma stopped eating, with her spoon halfway to her mouth. Mandy stopped talking. Adam forgot to watch what he was cooking. "It was difficult to hear," said Richard, "but someone was talking about Mrs Turnip, and asking if Adam would like to have her treasure."

"*Me?*" squeaked Adam.

"Yes," said Richard. "It was definitely your name. The person said something about it being rather dirty and would you care for it."

Adam looked at Mandy. "Why would Mrs Turnip give me some treasure?" he asked.

"Perhaps it's something to do with the pirate," said Mandy, "you know, her great uncle who went to sea."

"Yes," said Adam. "That must be it.

Perhaps this house was a pirate's hide-out."
He blew out the flames on his toast.

"This sounds exciting!" said Mrs Inchley.
"What did you say?"

"Well," said Richard, "I said yes, of
course. And the person said they'd be along
later."

Everyone started talking again. Adam
asked Mandy how she thought you cared
for treasure. Richard asked if Adam
wanted any help with it, and could he have
a share. Mr Inchley wondered if they'd
have to sell it to pay for a new kitchen
when Adam burnt theirs down with his
toast.

"Come on now everyone," said Mrs
Inchley. "That's enough talk. Let's finish
breakfast." Adam and Mandy finished
first. They jumped around the kitchen in
excitement until Mr Inchley started mutter-
ing about the washing-up. Then they went
into the living-room to watch for a car.

"I wonder what the treasure will be?"
said Adam.

"It could be gold, or diamonds," said Mandy, "and they're probably very dusty. Richard said it was dirty."

"Jewels," said Adam, "that we'll have to polish."

They spent the rest of the morning talking about the treasure and waiting for someone to arrive.

"Look!" said Mandy. "There's a car slowing down." The car stopped outside the house. A woman got out, leading a scruffy-looking dog. She disappeared around the side of the house.

"She's going to your back door," said Mandy. "I wonder what she wants?"

48

"Perhaps they've got the wrong house," said Adam. "I hope they move their car before the treasure arrives."

The woman didn't appear again, and the car was still outside. Adam and Mandy went to see what was going on.

As soon as Adam opened the kitchen door he knew something was wrong. It was very quiet, and there was a funny kind of smell. A dog was sitting in the middle of the room. It was a fat, grumpy-looking dog. Its long fur needed brushing and it looked as if it had been rolling in something nasty.

It was not very beautiful.

"Adam," said Mr Inchley, in an odd voice, "meet Treasure!"

For a moment Adam couldn't talk at all, then he said, "Treasure! This isn't treasure. Treasure is something nice!"

"Adam," said his mother, "Treasure is Mrs Turnip's dog. Mrs Turnip fell over in her cottage and hurt herself. No one found her for a long time, and she's very ill. She's got to stay in hospital."

"He doesn't look like a very nice dog," said Mandy.

The lady who'd brought Treasure said, "Mrs Turnip's bad leg made it difficult to care for her dog, and she's very upset about it. Her cottage is out on the marsh, a long way from the road, and Treasure's been roaming about on his own. Mrs Turnip asked me to bring him here. She would like you to have him, Adam. She thinks you'll look after him properly."

"I don't want her dog," said Adam. "I want a puppy."

"You did say you'd have Treasure," said his father.

Adam turned to his brother. "Why didn't you say Treasure was a dog?" he demanded.

"I didn't know," said Richard. "There was so much noise, I didn't hear everything."

"You have to keep him, Adam," said Mrs Inchley. "There isn't anyone else to care for him, and Mrs Turnip is relying on you."

"But Mum," said Adam, "I prayed for a puppy, and I trusted God to give me what I wanted."

"Sometimes, Adam," said his father gently, "when we ask God for things, he gives us what we need, not what we want."

Adam looked at the scruffy animal sitting on their floor. If this was God's idea of what he needed, thought Adam, it wasn't very funny. If he had this dog there would be no chance of having a puppy, not for years and years. Adam hadn't known he could feel so miserable.

Chapter 7

Don't look now, it's that dog

"Keep still, you silly dog!" said Mandy. They were shampooing Treasure. Mrs Inchley said the dog was so smelly that he had to have a wash before anything else.

First of all, Mandy and Adam had taken Treasure for a walk along the beach and tried to get him to go in the sea. Treasure didn't mind walking beside them, but he refused to go anywhere near the water. He wouldn't run with them, either. When Adam found a stick and threw it, Treasure looked at Adam as if to say, "You threw it, you can fetch it!" and sat down on the beach.

Mandy and Adam had to carry Treasure back to the house. This was not a pleasant thing to do. "Poo!" said Mandy. "He's dreadful! We'll just have to bath him."

So there they all were, in the bathroom. The three of them were very wet, and it was difficult to tell who looked the most cross, Treasure or Adam. The water in the bath was the colour of mud.

"I hope no one expects *me* to bath in here again," said Adam. Richard came in with some old towels.

"Mum sent these," he said. "Gosh,

Adam, not even *you* make this much dirt, even after football."

"Huh!" said Adam. "Instead of making comments, you can help us lift this dog out of the water." Richard helped them to lift out the dripping animal. The minute Treasure's feet touched the ground, he ran for the door.

"Stop him!" shouted Richard. "He'll make everything wet." Adam threw himself at the dog, trying to catch him with a rugby tackle. Treasure slid through his arms and Adam landed in a heap on the floor.

"Treasure," he shouted, "Come back here!"

The dog raced down the stairs and into the living-room, then he stopped in the middle of the carpet and shook himself. A shower of water went all over Mr and Mrs Inchley. Adam limped into the room, rubbing his leg.

"Why didn't you call him, Adam?" asked Mr Inchley, wiping his wet clothes.

"I DID," said Adam. "He didn't take any notice of me. I'm not calling this dog 'Treasure' again, whatever Mrs Turnip thinks. This dog isn't a treasure. This dog's horrid!"

"How about calling him Toby?" asked Mandy as she came in. "I read a story about a dog called Toby once. He was a nice dog in the end."

"All right," said Adam. "Toby's better than Treasure, but it'll take more than a new name to make this thing nice."

It seemed as if Adam was right. Toby got himself into lots of trouble. He stole Richard's sandwiches out of his bag and he made a bed out of Mr Inchley's best jumper.

He tipped all the rubbish out of the dustbin and he chewed up letters when they came through the letter-box. He barked at the dustmen and he chased any cat in sight. Adam got very tired of dragging Toby home and saying "sorry" for him.

One day Adam and Mandy took Toby to the sweet shop with them. Dogs weren't allowed inside, but there was a heavy waste paper bin just outside the door.

"Let's tie his lead to this," suggested Mandy.

"Good idea," said Adam. The bin had a big lump of concrete on the bottom, and they were sure Toby couldn't move it. They were wrong. Toby could.

Just as Adam was choosing what he wanted to buy, there was a dreadful noise. People in the shop crowded to the window to see what was happening. Mandy and Adam ran to the window, too, and they could hardly believe their eyes. A cat was running up the road with Toby galloping after it as fast as he could go. The bin had fallen on its side, Toby was dragging it behind him and rubbish was blowing all over the road. Everyone was stopping to look. Mandy and Adam felt dreadfully embarrassed. Adam wished the ground would open and swallow him up, or better still, swallow up Toby.

That evening Mandy and Emma were sitting with Adam and Richard in front of a fire in the living-room, reading their Bibles. Their parents were very keen on Bible reading, and the family read together every week. Mandy and Adam had a booklet to help them. It included games and puzzles about the Bible, so the reading was really fun to do.

"Do you think God wants us to forgive dogs as well as people?" asked Mandy that evening.

"That's a funny question," said Emma.

"Our Bible reading's about forgiving people," Mandy explained, "and I wondered if it meant forgiving dogs, too." Adam looked up from a puzzle he was finishing. "If I've got to forgive Toby for what he did today," he said, "I'll use up all my forgivingness in one go."

Emma laughed. She gave Toby a pat. "He can't be that bad," she said.

Mandy told her what had happened at the shop. "We had to chase Toby all the way down the road," she said, "*and* collect up the rubbish."

"It was horrible," said Adam. "You needn't laugh, Richard. It wasn't funny.

Everyone was watching. I really hate that dog."

"That's a shame," said Dr West, coming in to say hello. She'd just got back from the hospital.

"How's Mrs Turnip getting on?" asked Emma.

"She's still very poorly," said Dr West. "I don't think she'd be getting better at all if she was worried about her dog. She's very grateful to you for giving him a home, Adam. It's a shame you don't like him."

"I suppose it's not his fault," said Adam. "He's used to running around by himself." And he thought, I suppose I can forgive Toby, but I'm still angry with God. Why has he done this to me? It's just not fair.

Chapter 8

Hello, Christmas ...

"Do you two want to come with me today?" Mrs Inchley asked Adam and Mandy. "I'm going to feed the animals." It was Christmas Eve. The college where Mrs Inchley worked had goats and sheep and even a calf. They had smaller animals like rabbits, too, and some geese and chickens. Although the students were at home for the holidays, the animals still needed to be fed.

"I'd like to come," said Mandy. "Mum and Dad won't be back for ages." Mandy's parents were doing some last minute Christmas shopping. She and Adam were busy finishing a present for Mrs Turnip.

Emma had taken a photograph of Toby and they were making it into a calendar.

"Toby could come with us," said Mrs Inchley.

"Oh, Mum," said Adam, "he's always getting into trouble."

"Mrs Turnip says he's used to animals," said his mother.

"I'll help you keep an eye on him," said Mandy. "He'll enjoy running around the fields."

Mandy put Toby on his lead and Mrs Inchley got the car out of the garage. Toby liked riding in the car. He sat up on the back seat and looked out of the window.

"I hope the geese stay on their pond this time," said Adam. "They always attack me."

When they arrived, Mrs Inchley and Mandy went off to get the food for the animals. As soon as Adam got out of the car, the geese left their pond and began to walk towards him. They stretched out their necks, opening their beaks and hissing at him.

"Oh-oh," said Adam. "Here we go again!" He waved his arms and shouted at them, but the geese kept coming. Just before they got close enough to peck Adam's legs, Toby ran to his defence. He jumped between Adam and the birds, giving sharp, warning barks. The geese scurried back to their pond.

Toby wagged his tail.

"Thank you, Toby," said Adam. "I didn't know you could do anything that useful."

"What a clever dog," said Mandy, coming back with Mrs Inchley. "I've got my hands full with this bowl of sheep food or I'd give you a pat!"

Of all the animals, Mandy and Adam liked the sheep best. They were a special kind of sheep called Jacob's, with long, curly horns. "If you two feed the sheep for me," said Mrs Inchley, "that'll be a real help. But stay away from the ram."

"We have to be careful of Derby the ram," said Adam. "He's not very friendly."

"He looks pretty fierce," said Mandy.

"Mum told me that rams sometimes kill people," said Adam. "She doesn't like us to go into his field."

Mandy and Adam spent the rest of the morning helping to feed the animals. Toby followed them around, sniffing at all the interesting smells, but for once he didn't get into any trouble.

"It's kind of nice, feeding animals at Christmas time," said Adam. "It makes me think of the shepherds."

"Yes," said Mandy. "These sheep are very friendly. You could imagine what it would have been like, keeping watch over them all night."

"And then the angels, and going to find Jesus," said Adam.

"Christmas is one of my favourite times of the year," Mandy agreed.

"I'll just put the rest of the food away, then we'll go," said Mrs Inchley. "We'll pop into the hospital to say hello to Mrs Turnip." On the way back to the car the geese hissed at Adam, but Toby was close behind him, so they stayed on their pond.

At the hospital Mrs Turnip was very pleased to see them.

"Bless you, m'dears!" she said, when Mrs Inchley apologised for arriving covered in straw and smelling of sheep. "Don't you worry about that. It's good to have a breath of country air." Mrs Turnip was getting better, but she still couldn't walk, and didn't know when she could go back to her cottage. She liked the present that Mandy and Adam had made her.

"And how's Treasure?" she asked, with a twinkle in her eye. It was the first time

Adam had been able to say that the dog had been good.

Toby kept on being good all through Christmas Eve, but he made up for it in a big way on Christmas Day.

Chapter 9

... Goodbye, dinner!

Adam woke up early on Christmas morning. He crept out of bed and pulled up the string he kept hanging down through the trapdoor. He used it to get things up and down, and sure enough there was a Christmas stocking on the end, full of interesting bulges. Adam felt the lumps carefully and tried to guess what they were before he opened them. Then he found his other presents, and opened them. He could smell the turkey cooking downstairs, and he had to have some of the chocolate from his stocking to stop his stomach from rumbling.

After that he got dressed to take Toby for a run on the beach. He slid down the rope ladder onto the landing. The smell of turkey was very strong there and Adam could hear his father downstairs in the kitchen.

Mr and Mrs Inchley had had a lively argument about the turkey the day before. It was very big, and Mrs Inchley wanted to leave it cooking while they were all at church, but Mr Inchley wouldn't hear of it.

"We'd have to leave the oven on," he'd said, "and it's a wooden house. Think of the fire risk! We might not have a home to come back to."

"If we don't cook it until we get back," Mrs Inchley had said, "we'll be eating lunch at tea time. And I'm not getting up in the middle of the night to cook it." In the end Adam's father said *he'd* get up early to put it in the oven, which is what he did.

"Happy Christmas, Dad," said Adam as he collected Toby.

"Happy Christmas!" said his father. "Yes, please take that animal out. He thinks he's helping."

When Adam and Toby got back, everyone else was in the kitchen. The turkey was on a plate on top of the stove.

"Come on," said Mr Inchley. "Hurry up and finish breakfast. We don't want to be late for church."

"We'd better make sure Toby's shut out of the kitchen while we're out," said Mrs Inchley. "His nose has been twitching all morning."

When everyone was in the car ready to go, Richard remembered he'd left his music on the kitchen table. He rushed back in for it.

The Christmas service was noisy and fun, with everyone singing carols at the top of their voices. The little children held up their presents for everybody to see, then they all said thank you for Jesus, the best present of all. At the end, people stood around shaking hands and hugging each other and saying "Happy Christmas!" Then everyone went home for dinner.

Emma was the first one into the kitchen. "Oh, no! I don't believe it!" she said.

Mr Inchley was next. "You terrible animal!" he shouted.

Mrs Inchley peered over his shoulder.

"Oh, Toby, what have you done?" she asked.

Toby was lying on the floor. He had an enormous bulge in his middle, and pieces of the turkey were scattered around him.

"Has that dog eaten our food?" asked Richard. "Throw him in the sea! Feed him to the fish!" Toby looked very sorry. He crawled underneath the table and he looked so miserable that Adam said, "It's not his fault. He doesn't know it's wrong." Just then, in walked Mandy with Dr and Mr

West. They'd been invited back for coffee. Mr West started to laugh.

"Oh, my," he said. "Looks like turkey's not on your menu today!"

"I don't know what else we've got to eat," said Mrs Inchley. "I can't think how he got into the kitchen. I'm sure I shut the door on the way out." She looked at Richard. Richard turned red and went very quiet.

"Don't worry," said Dr West. "Come back to our house. We've got a turkey, and my aunt filled our freezer with Jamaican food when she was here."

"Yes," said Mandy. "We could have a real feast." So that is what they did, and everyone enjoyed themselves very much. When Mandy said she was glad that Toby had eaten the Inchleys' turkey, not even Richard disagreed.

"At least life's never boring with Toby around," said Adam, and no one disagreed with that, either.

Chapter 10

A Ram Called Derby

After Christmas, winter seemed to go on for ever. Adam hated getting up for school in the dark, but he liked taking Toby for a run in the snow. At last the weather got warmer. It was the beginning of spring, and at Mrs Inchley's college the first lambs were born.

"Can Jack come with us today?" asked Adam, one Saturday just before Easter. "He wanted to play football but I said we were going to see the lambs."

"Jack can come if he wants to," said Mrs Inchley. "Tell him we'll pick him up when we collect Mandy."

Jack was waiting for them outside his house. He had a football in his hands.

"You'll have to share the back seat with me and Toby," said Adam, opening the car door.

"I don't mind," said Jack. "Your dog's much better at behaving now."

"I think he's been better since his fur was clipped," said Mandy. "He's got to live up to his good looks."

"He's still a bit hairy," said Adam. "Move over, Toby. It's a good job we're not going very far."

The three of them spent the journey

talking about the Easter holidays.

"What I don't understand," said Jack, "is why the Friday before Easter is called *Good* Friday. Isn't that the day that Jesus died? What can be good about that?"

"We think it's good because he died for us," said Mandy.

"It's not easy to explain," said Mrs Inchley. "Jesus is God, and he didn't have to die. We're the ones who have done wrong, but he died instead of us. He sort of took our place."

"I still don't understand it," said Jack.

"Come to Easter Holiday Club at church," said Mandy. "They'll tell you all about it."

"It's fun," agreed Adam. "We go sailing as well."

"I wish we had our own boat," said Mandy. Adam nodded.

"We're nearly there," said Mrs Inchley.

"Wait till you see the lambs, Jack," said Adam. "They're really cute."

The lambs were tiny and very soft. Three of them were really small, and needed extra food. Adam, Mandy and Jack held the little creatures in their arms and fed them with milk from a bottle like a baby's feeding bottle. The lambs drank thirstily, wagging their tails and butting with their heads.

When they had finished drinking, Adam lifted them back into the pen with the other sheep.

Mrs Inchley was feeding the other animals. She was on her way to Derby's field when someone called her to the telephone.

"I've got to take a phone call," she said. "If you three have finished, just wait by the car. I won't be long."

"Let's play football while we're waiting," said Mandy.

"Good idea," said Adam.

Across from the car park, beside Derby's field, there was a flattish bit of grass big enough for a kick-about. They chose a place for the goal, and Adam said he'd be keeper. The sun was shining, and they had great fun. Toby was sniffing around the edge of Derby's field, where the ram was watching them unhappily over his low fence. Derby was not happy. Mrs Inchley hadn't fed him but she'd put his food down where he could see it, and smell it. He just couldn't reach it. Derby pawed the grass angrily.

"Goal!" shouted Mandy, getting one past Adam. "Here comes another!" said Jack. He gave the ball a hefty kick. It sailed high in the air, a beautiful, curving shot.

Adam watched as it floated down, down, down: then a gust of wind caught the ball and carried it over the fence. It landed smack on Derby.

"I'll get it!" said Jack. The fence had a big wooden sign on it that said: *Danger. Beware of the Ram!* but Jack took no notice of this. Before Mandy or Adam could stop him, he climbed into the field.

"Jack!" shouted Adam. "No! Come back!" Jack turned and waved, and Adam saw the ram look up. Derby was hot, cross and hungry. He watched as Jack walked towards the football, then he got ready to charge.

For a moment, Adam and Mandy were so shocked that they stood like statues, unable to move. Then Adam came back to life, and without stopping to think, he climbed over the fence and ran towards Derby, shouting at the top of his voice.

"Come on, stupid animal," he yelled. "Try and catch me!" Derby turned to Adam. He snorted angrily and at last Jack saw the danger he was in. He scrambled quickly away, out of sight of the ram. As soon as Adam was sure Jack was safe, he began to run himself, back to the edge of the field. His heart was pounding with fear.

It felt like a mile to the fence and his legs seemed to be going forever, but at last Adam was there – the railing was in his grasp. He started to climb. Thank goodness, he thought. I'm safe. But when he tried to pull his foot out of the mesh to swing himself to safety, he couldn't move. His lace had got tangled in some loose wire. He couldn't get it free. Adam was trapped, spread across the fence like a target, and the ram was beginning to charge.

Chapter 11

Toby to the rescue

Adam pulled at his shoe and tugged at his foot. He looked up to see Derby rushing towards him, the massive horns pointed straight at his chest. Adam's eyes opened wide in horror and he scrabbled to undo his lace, his fingers stiff with terror.

"Mum!" he heard himself calling, "Mum! Mum!" but she was too far away. Adam thought, she'll never get to me in time. I'll be crushed against the wire. I'm going to die.

At that moment he saw a blur of black and white. It was Toby, running at full speed towards the slope behind the field.

He raced up the bank and launched himself into the air, cleared the fence with one jump and ran straight for the ram.

Toby crouched in front of the furious animal, barking madly. For a moment Adam thought Derby was still going to attack him, but at the last minute the ram turned away, snorting and tossing his head angrily.

At last Adam's foot was free. He scrambled over the fence, then turned in horror to see the ram scoop Toby up with his horns.

Adam watched, helpless, as Derby tossed his head, flinging the dog into the air. Toby crashed to the earth. His body landed with a thud and he lay without moving.

Meanwhile, Mandy had grabbed Derby's food. She opened the gate and ran across the field, calling his name and shaking the bowl to make the food rattle. Derby snorted and stamped his hooves, but he trotted after Mandy. She led the ram to his shed and put his food on the floor. As soon as he was inside, eating, Mandy slammed the door. Her fingers shook as she pushed the bolt across.

Jack had gone to fetch Mrs Inchley. When she understood what was happening she hurried back anxiously. "Adam, Mandy, are you all right?" she called.

Adam was kneeling on the grass beside Toby. He nodded silently. "That was such a brave thing to do!" said his mother, giving him a hug. She turned and smiled at Mandy. "You did exactly right, Mandy," she said.

"Mum," said Adam urgently, "Toby's hurt. What's wrong with him? I can't get him to wake up." Toby lay very still. He looked like a limp toy, not like a real dog at all.

Mrs Inchley felt for a pulse in Toby's neck, then she said, "I'll ring for the vet. You and Mandy stay here," and she walked quickly away.

Mandy knelt next to Adam. "Oh, Toby," she said. "Brave dog! Please wake up." She ran her fingers along Toby's head, stroking the silky fur, touching the still face.

Adam picked up the dog's limp paw, holding it gently, feeling the soft pads between his fingers. He remembered times when he and Mandy had tried to get Toby to shake hands. "Don't die," he said. "Please don't die ..."

The earth around them was flattened, trampled by the ram. The field was full of thistles and small stones, but Adam didn't notice them digging into his knees. He knelt beside Toby's body, willing him to live, wanting him to open his eyes.

Jack stood helplessly on one side, shifting from leg to leg. He looked at Adam, trying to think of something to say.

"If he dies," Jack said finally, "well, if he does die, at least you can have your puppy. I'm sure your mum would get you a puppy now."

Adam looked up. "I don't want a puppy!" he said. "I only want Toby. I just didn't know till now how much I *do* want him," and he bent his head to hide his tears.

"Adam," his mum's voice was gentle as

she walked back across the field towards them. "I've called the vet and he's coming as soon as he can." She looked at Jack. "I've rung your dad and he said he'll come and fetch you," she told him. "I'm sure you'll feel better at home. Do you want to go back with them, Mandy?"

Mandy shook her head. "No thank you," she said, "I want to stay here, with Toby."

"Is he all right Mum?" said Adam. "He's going to be all right, isn't he?"

"He's very sick, Adam," said Mrs Inchley, "but the vet will be here soon."

Jack bent over Toby and stroked him, not quite knowing what to say. "I'm sorry," he said at last, "I hope he'll be all right."

Adam nodded, not trusting himself to speak. Why didn't the vet come? It seemed ages since his mum had gone to phone. Why wasn't he here NOW? Toby needed him so badly.

His mother was standing quietly, with her head bowed, and Adam knew she was praying.

It's just as well Mum's talking to God, thought Adam. I shouldn't think it's any use *me* praying. I said some awful things when Toby first arrived and I don't think God will listen to me now. I don't expect he'll ever listen to me again.

Chapter 12

Happy Easter?

Jack's father arrived to take Jack home, and the vet arrived soon afterwards. He looked very serious, and took Toby away with him to the animal hospital.

Everyone thought Adam and Mandy were really brave, and they were treated like heroes.

They even had their pictures in the paper. Dr West said they'd probably be suffering from shock and she gave them hot, sweet drinks. She sent Mandy to bed and put Adam in their guest room so that she could keep an eye on them both. They didn't enjoy the fuss, and when Adam went home the next day, his house seemed terribly empty. No one would tell them if Toby was going to get well.

School finished, and Adam and Mandy really missed their dog.

"It's Easter day tomorrow," said Adam. "It doesn't feel like Easter."

"No," said Mandy. "I'm sure Toby's going to die. I don't think I've ever been so unhappy."

It was a very quiet group of people who went to church next day. Mrs Inchley had to go to her college to feed the animals and Adam stood close to his dad, feeling a bit lost. Easter was usually such a happy time, but everything seemed unreal this year.

After the service Mrs Inchley was waiting

for them outside. "Mandy and her family are coming to lunch with us," she said. "There's a surprise waiting for you at home." Adam guessed she meant Easter eggs, but when he and Mandy got to the house they could hardly believe their eyes.

The biggest parcel they'd ever seen was sitting in the passage between their house and the one next door. It was covered in gift paper and filled the whole space like the giant, flat egg of some incredible bird.

"Whatever can it be?" said Mandy.

"I can't guess," said Adam, interested in something for the first time that week.

"Come inside," said Mrs Inchley. "Something's waiting for you in here, too."

And there in the middle of the floor, wagging his tail as if it would come off and grinning wobbly doggy grins was – Toby!

"Toby!" Adam and Mandy swooped down on him, laughing and hugging him.

"Be gentle!" said Mrs Inchley. "He's had an operation. Don't squeeze him too hard." When they'd finished saying hello they all went out to investigate the strange parcel. Toby had to come too, and he helped to pull off the paper when they started to unwrap it. Mr and Mrs Inchley, Emma, Richard, Dr and Mr West all crowded into the passage to watch.

"It's a boat!" said Mandy as the paper came off. "A real sailing boat!" She rushed to hug her mum and dad.

"It's for both of you," said Mr West. "You were so brave and sensible that we thought we'd get you something to show you both how proud we are."

"Toby's the bravest," said Mandy.

"We'd better take him sailing with us," said Adam. "How do you fancy being a sea dog, Toby?"

The rest of Easter was great. Mr West helped them to launch their boat and then took them for a sail. It was a good day after all, but at church that evening Adam was very quiet. When they all got back, he went out and stood on the balcony by himself, thinking. Emma's door opened and she went to lean on the railing with him.

"What's wrong, Adam?" she asked. "I was watching you in church this evening, and you looked really sad. Is anything the matter? I thought everything was all right now."

"It's church," said Adam. "I shouldn't have been there. Everyone was so happy, saying thank you to Jesus, and he can't want me there. I said some terrible things when he gave me Mrs Turnip's dog, and he was right all the time. A puppy wouldn't have been used to sheep, and I might have been killed."

"God understood how you felt, Adam. He still cares about you. You said some awful things to Toby, too, and he still likes you, doesn't he?"

"Toby really loves me," said Adam, "and I don't deserve it. I hated him, and called him names, but he loves me anyway."

"Yes, he does," said Emma, "and you need to know that God loves you like that, too."

"God can't love me as much as Toby does," said Adam. "Toby was prepared to give his life for me." Emma looked at him without speaking for a moment, then she smiled.

"Happy Easter, Adam," she said.

I wonder if you know what she meant.

Other titles in the Read by Myself series

Message in a bottle
Heather Butler

Robert's heart was beating extra fast. As he reached the porch he paused. This was it!
This was the start of his plan.
This could be good.
Or it could be the end of him doing the milk-round – if ever Dad found out.

Robert helps his dad with the milk-round on Saturdays, and he starts sending messages to Alf who owns a large model train track. What is the secret of Oak Lodge? Puzzles, secret codes and jokes form part of the story.

My Real Rabbit
Geraldine Witcher

At the week-end, Mum said, "I think a boy who is too old for Peter Rabbit might be old enough for a real rabbit. Don't you think so, Mike?"
Mike stared.
"Yes please!" Mike couldn't believe it. A real rabbit of his very own! Mike wants to be grown-up, but he discovers that a real rabbit is quite a handful!

Discovering the Bible with Scripture Union

In *Mrs Turnip's Treasure*, Adam and Mandy enjoyed using their Bible reading notes. You will too!

Let's Go is for 7s and 8s – a colour magazine that helps you discover the Bible.

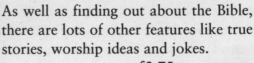

Travel through time with Jack, Tara, Ratty, Walls and Boff the Prof as they meet characters from Bible stories. **£2.75 per quarter.**

Check it Out! is the ultimate Bible reading guide for 9s to 11s. Every three months there are pages to pull out and file in the special **Check it Out!** binder.

As well as finding out about the Bible, there are lots of other features like true stories, worship ideas and jokes.
£2.75 per quarter.
£5.99 for the binder.

Available from your local Christian bookshop, or in case of difficulty please contact Scripture Union Mail Order, PO Box 764, Oxford. OX4 5JF.